WATERSHIP™ DOWN

Primrose's Great Escape

Diane Redmond

RED FOX

A Red Fox Book

Published by Random House Children's Books
20 Vauxhall Bridge Road, London SW1V 2SA

A division of The Random House Group Ltd
London Melbourne Sydney Auckland
Johannesburg and agencies throughout the world

Text and illustrations © 2000 Alltime Entertainment Ltd.

www.watershipdown.net

Illustrations by County Studio, Leicester

1 3 5 7 9 10 8 6 4 2

Printed and bound in Italy

THE RANDOM HOUSE GROUP Limited Reg. No. 954009

www.randomhouse.co.uk

ISBN 0 09 940809 0

This story represents scenes from the television series, Watership Down,
which is inspired by Richard Adams' novel of the same name.

In the gloomy warren of Efrafa, Bigwig was standing in front of General Woundwort.

'I have travelled far to find a new leader,' he said.

Woundwort looked down from his high platform.

'We take only strong rabbits here,' he growled.
'Can you fight?'

Bigwig nodded. 'I was the best in my warrren.'

Woundwort pointed to one of his guards.

'Then fight Vervain,' he ordered.

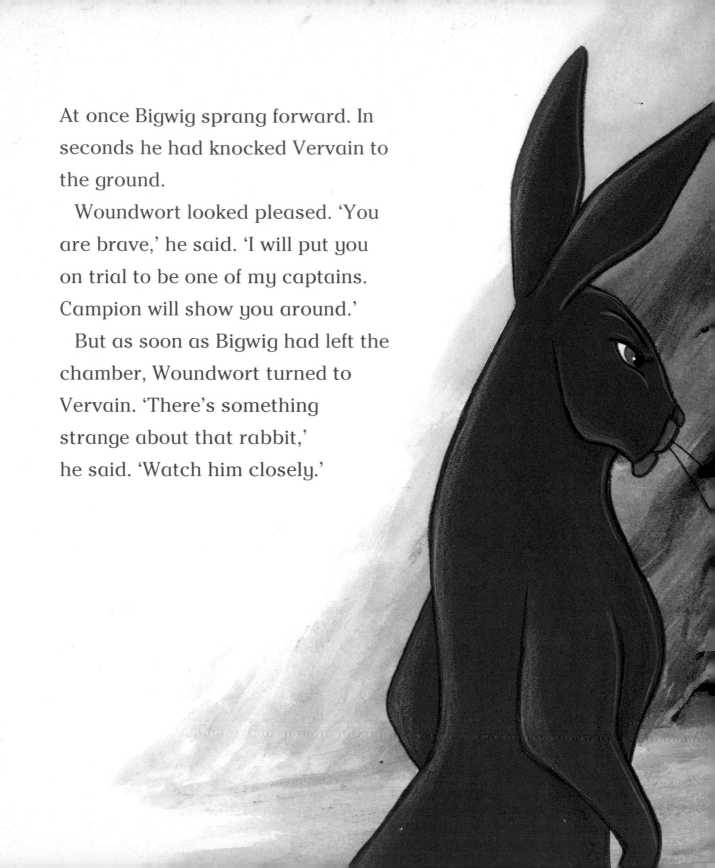

At once Bigwig sprang forward. In seconds he had knocked Vervain to the ground.

Woundwort looked pleased. 'You are brave,' he said. 'I will put you on trial to be one of my captains. Campion will show you around.'

But as soon as Bigwig had left the chamber, Woundwort turned to Vervain. 'There's something strange about that rabbit,' he said. 'Watch him closely.'

Not far from Efrafa, Hazel, Fiver and Hawkbit were hiding under an old stone bridge.

'I can't believe Bigwig has just disappeared,' grumbled Hawkbit. 'We've come to rescue Primrose.'

Hazel was more concerned about the guards on the bridge above. 'If they're here when we escape,' he said. 'We'll be trapped.'

Just then Blackberry appeared. 'Come and look at this,' she said. 'I think I've found our escape route.'

Hazel followed Blackberry along the bank to where a small boat was tied. He looked at the boat, not sure what to think.

Then Fiver hopped up. 'With this boat thing, we won't need the bridge,' he explained. 'We can float away!'

Suddenly Fiver froze. 'Someone's coming,' he whispered. 'Hide!'

The rabbits dived for cover, but the next minute they heard a familiar voice.

Bigwig had hopped onto the bridge, and was peering down a hole in the middle of it. 'There's a bit of a problem with security here, but nothing we can't sort out,' he said, winking at Hazel. 'I think I'm going to enjoy being in Efrafa.'

'Good,' said Campion. 'We need strong rabbits like you.'

Hazel turned to his friends. 'Bigwig's on the inside!' he gasped.

Moments after Bigwig and Campion had left the bridge, Vervain marched up.

'What was Bigwig doing here?' he asked one of the guards.

'He talked about security and looked at a hole in the bridge.'

'A hole?' said Vervain. 'Show it to me at once!'

Under the bridge Fiver started to tremble. 'He's going to see us,' he said.

But before Vervain could look down the hole, Kehaar flew straight up through it, knocking him over. When Vervain got up and started to run for home, Kehaar followed him, shrieking loudly.

Back in Efrafa, Campion told Bigwig to look around on his
own while he went off to supervise some burrow digging.

The big rabbit moved slowly down the dark passage until
he found the chamber where Primrose and Blackavar slept.
'Hello, I'm Bigwig,' he said. 'Hazel sent me to help you escape.'

Primrose smiled. 'We're ready,' she said and, pulling aside
a thick root, revealed the entrance to a tunnel. 'I dug it
myself. It leads to the embankment behind the guards.'

Bigwig looked impressed. 'Hazel was right about you,' he
said. 'We'll leave tonight, just before sunset.'

Bigwig went outside to look around. As he came close to some bushes, he heard a rustling noise.

'Bigwig, it's me,' whispered Hazel. 'We've found a way to escape, if you can make it to the stone bridge.'

Bigwig pretended to eat some grass. 'See the sentry over there?'

Hazel looked out from his hiding place. 'Yes, I can see him.'

'We'll be coming out of a tunnel behind him tonight,' said Bigwig.

But before Hazel could reply, Vervain came up with two guards. 'You're under arrest,' he told Bigwig. 'General Woundwort wants a word with you.'

Inside Woundwort's council
chamber, Vervain jumped up.
'Bigwig's in league with a gull,'
he told the general. 'The same one
that once helped Hazel and Fiver
escape from here.'

'A gull?' laughed Bigwig. 'That's quite
a story. You're just jealous because
I beat you in a fight. Well I've had
enough of you.' And he leapt on Vervain.

'Hold the prisoner!' roared Woundwort
to his guards. Then he went across to
Bigwig and slashed his shoulder
with his sharp claws. 'Your trial
is over, Captain Bigwig. I think
you will do well in Efrafa.'

Bigwig left the council chamber and ran quickly to Primrose. 'We must leave now!' he said. 'Vervain has guessed who I am.'

Primrose lifted the root and they all went into the escape tunnel.

Above, Vervain was pacing up and down, on guard duty. By chance he trod on the tunnel entrance and landed with a crash – face to face with Bigwig. 'Escape!' he shouted. 'Guards, come quickly!'

Vervain struck out, but Bigwig ducked and kicked Vervain against the wall of the tunnel, sending a shower of earth on top of him.

'Our escape route's blocked!' cried Bigwig. 'Run back the way we came!'

In the bushes outside, Hazel, Fiver and Hawkbit were
waiting. Suddenly they heard a crashing noise and saw
Bigwig charging towards them, with Primrose and
Blackavar.

'It's Bigwig!' cried Fiver. 'They made it!'

'But Woundwort's on their trail,' said Hazel. 'Run quickly!'

The rabbits bolted at once. They raced through the woods, closely followed by Woundwort and his guards, until at last they reached the bridge.

'Head for the river!' cried Hazel, scrambling down the bank.

When Woundwort saw where the rabbits were going, he smiled. 'They're trapped,' he snarled. 'Bring them to me.'

Underneath the bridge Blackberry was chewing on the boat rope. Fiver, Hawkbit, Primrose and Blackavar dived onto the boat, leaving Hazel and Bigwig on the bank to face the guards.

'I'm sorry it had to end this way!' said Campion, as the Efrafans closed in.

Suddenly the rope snapped and the boat started to move. Hazel and Bigwig turned and raced along the bank. With a leap they landed in the boat.

'They're getting away on the river!' said Campion in surprise.

'No!' roared Woundwort and dived in after them.

Swiftly, Bigwig kicked him away. 'Sorry, Woundwort, we're full up. Get your own boat!' he laughed.

Hazel and Primrose sat together at the front of the boat, as it drifted gently down the river.

'I was so afraid,' said Primrose.

Hazel smiled into her eyes. 'You don't need to be afraid any more,' he whispered. 'You're free!'